Tales of an
African Boy

MALIK

Written by Mary Lindop and illustrated by Michelle Dahl

AuthorHouse™
1663 Liberty Drive
Bloomington, IN 47403
www.authorhouse.com
Phone: 833-262-8899

Interior Image Credit: Michelle Dahl

This book is printed on acid-free paper.

ISBN: 979-8-8230-4172-0 (sc)
ISBN: 979-8-8230-4174-4 (hc)
ISBN: 979-8-8230-4173-7 (e)

Library of Congress Control Number: 2025901124

Print information available on the last page.

Published by AuthorHouse 01/21/2025

authorHOUSE®

To every child reading this book,

Know that you are of greatness.

Don't let disappointments or others

Hold you back.

You have a destiny to fulfill!

ACKNOWLEDGEMENTS

The privilege of writing this book has been an extraordinary one. This endeavor has been out of this author's love for children (our future).

Acknowledgements and my thanks are due the following people who provided many helpful editing tips and comments: to Marquita Walker, Michelle Dahl and Dale Blyden.

I would like to add an extra word of love and appreciation to my children and grandchildren. They are my legacy and my hope for the future.

FOREWORD

This book is an historical fiction about a young Mandinka boy, Malik, and his journey to become a great Mandinka leader. The wording in these stories and the pictures in this collection have been introduced in an attempt to bring the past to life.

The passing down of oral history through music is one of the most distinctive traits of the Mandinka. As Malik drums, the words of his ancestors come to him and he is taught many valuable life lessons.

These five tales are full of symbolism and personification as the jungle creatures are brought to life. Through the characters you will experience levels of emotions such as empathy, love, compassion, fear and trepidation. Their interactions provide the opportunity for meaningful discussions related to character, beliefs, morality, and ethics.

CONTENTS

I   **Mawee and the Tribe of Birds** *(a tale of finding our spirit, unification, and strength in numbers)*..*1*

II   **Makumba: The Story of Mother Elephant** *(a tale of courage and leadership)* 9

III **The Tortoise and the Garden** *(a tale of power and reclaiming what is rightfully yours)* *15*

IV **Doobaloo, Khari and the Baby Chicks** *(a tale about protecting the children to preserve our future)*..*21*

V   **Taroo the Crow and the Stones of Wisdom** *(a tale providing words of wisdom to live by)* *29*

Mawee and the Tribe of Birds

In the great continent of Africa, in the village of Una, lived a young African boy with ebony skin, big round eyes, and a cheerful face. His name was Malik, which in the African language means "Divine." Malik lived in a small hut with his father, mother, and seven brothers. He was third born by birthright. Slender in stature but with great strength, this little boy of the Mandinka bloodline was fearless and brave.

Malik was drawn to the amazing creatures of Africa and he could talk in a secret language with them. The animals taught him life lessons, how to coexist with one another, living in peace and harmony. Malik also believed in the rhythm of the earth, of nature and its healing powers. For centuries, his tribe harnessed the powers of nature and the powers of African plant life to purify, heal and sustain their bodies. He was one with nature, and the Great Spirits of Africa were with him. He was gifted with powers beyond those in his tribe.

This little boy was full of both mischief and wisdom, a good combination for getting him into and out of trouble. Often, Malik was outside of his parents' reach and would many times be in danger of the wild animals and unfriendly neighboring tribes. He was never afraid though and knew he was always being watched and protected by the spirits of his ancestors. Malik came from a line of greatness, and one day he knew he would become a great Mandinka warrior like his father and grandfather.

Today was to be a very special occasion for Malik. It was his 13th birthday and Malik had just completed the rite of passage into manhood. He had lived for a time in the bush learning about plants and herbs for medicine, the wild animals, hunting for food, surviving in the jungle wilderness, and the roles and responsibilities of becoming a man of the Mandinka tribe. He had now passed the rite of passage and a celebration was in order. Food, dancing, and music for the festivity!

Malik dearly loved music and for this celebration, his father crafted him a Djembe; an ancient drum of the Mandinka people made from African wood and animal skins. To pass the time away, Malik played his new drum. He was moved by its sound and there was such love in Malik's heart for his people when he would beat his drum. When Malik would dance to the rhythm of the drum, he would immerse himself in the sounds of Africa: The trumpeting elephant, the grunt of the hippo, the laughing hyena, the roar of the lion, the crested falcons calling to each other, and the cicadas, lizards, and frogs.

Malik was schooled by the elders in his tribe, and was taught that when the Mandinka drummed, the words of their ancestors would come to them; their hearts, minds, and souls would be joined together. This pleased the elders and their spirits would come, bringing communion and filling all with wisdom and power.

Malik awoke the next morning to the nuzzling head of a baby goat. Outside of his hut, father's herd of goats was grazing on the grass. Just yesterday, before his journey into manhood, his job was to keep an eye on the herd making sure it did not wander away. Each goat was named and called if it went astray.

However, today, Malik has become a young Mandinka tribesman, stronger and braver, having gone through his rite of passage. It is now his responsibility to help protect the village from lions and water buffalo. He passes the day competing with the other young men in the tribe, chanting songs as they work together, learning the skills of becoming a Mandinka warrior.

As the day darkened into night, Malik sat by the fire and listened to the stories of the griots; elders who narrated stories about the history of the Mandinka people and bygone days. Malik played his drum and talked to his ancestors through the sound of his music. He spoke to them:

Gone from us

Out of sight

Take me back

To what's right

Hear me now

Come, bright light

Protect our ancient way of life.

That night, looking up at the stars in the heaven, Malik heard the wind whisper to him "Out of Africa they all came. The uttering of their names will unleash their spirits and your birthright will be revealed. You and your kin were created from greatness." Malik returned to the refuge of his small hut remembering the stories of the griots. With a sense of purpose and belonging, he fell into a deep sleep.

After a short time, a voice came to Malik saying, "I have heard the call of your drum." In his dream, Malik looked up to see an elderly black man of great light. The man said to Malik: "My name is Ykni and I am an elder of the lost tribes of Africa." Malik was at first fearful of this apparition, and responded "Why are you here? What have you come for?" Ykni said: "Do not be afraid. I have come because I am worried about the future of our people. They have lost touch with their ancestors and the traditions of the Mandinka. There has been great destruction of our family and tribe. I tell you the thoughts of my heart. In time mankind all lived together because it was not well for a person to be without family or tribe. Once you were born you became a member of a larger people. A people that provided sustenance, comfort, guidance, and support for each other."

Malik replied, "You are Wisdom," so I ask of you, "What is to become of our people?" Ykni answered saying, "We have a sacred link; Mandinka blood runs through your veins and our hearts are one. You are young and have much to learn. You will grow and one day take your father's place; you will sit in council on the highest seat. You will become a teacher and help to unify the 'Tribes of Africa'".

The powerful vision and prophecy of the elder troubled Malik as he was not ready for such a great task. Eventually, the unsettling night passed and day broke. The next morning, Malik awoke very fatigued, with a grumbling in his stomach. To lift his spirit and replenish his energy, he decided to go out and hunt for food. Malik picked up his spear and traveled into the forest where he saw a tribe of birds in the distance. They were numerous, dancing among the trees. Testing his new strength and skill, he thrust his spear into the band of wild birds striking one. The bird fell to the ground, stumbling around, squawking in distress. Malik approached the felled bird. When the bird finally stopped weeping and wailing, he was able to breathe easy and speak to Malik.

> "Listen to me and I will give you counsel. If you will spare my life, and mend my
> wing, I will teach you the knowledge of the end and the beginning of a village.
> Small as I am, I can teach you this wisdom."

Malik was vexed with the bird, but decided to do as it requested. Malik gently lifted the bird and washed its wound with water from the nearby river. He gathered pieces of vine to wrap around the broken wing and hold it in place so that it could heal. He placed the bird back on the ground and waited to see if it could walk. Malik told the bird it would take days for the wing to heal and he would take care of all its needs until it was able to fly again. Each day, Malik would go to the bird and bring him food and water.

Malik and the bird became very good friends. The bird told Malik he had not long lived in this forest. Long ago, they lived as a family of birds; they danced among the trees and sang the songs of their ancestors. They rejoiced with the coming of the new chicks and taught them the lessons of life. He was sad when man destroyed his forest and when his tribe had to move away to this distant land.

This place was now their new home. Here, the bird tribe lived among strangers and had to learn new ways to survive and be happy again. At first, they were slow-witted, not knowing the lay of the land or where to find food. One of the elder birds found a spring where mankind got their drinking water. Another was able to find trees with an abundance of ripened fruit. They had the essentials of life to sustain them, but they were still not happy. They could fly, feed, and nest in this small green forest, but they could not dwell together as they once did. Something was missing. Their lives had been diminished, they had lost their song, their dance, their hue of color, their kinship.

Malik, hearing the bird's story, was very sad. The bird said "Do not be sad Malik. I have not yet finished my story." The bird went on to tell Malik that one day while all the birds were feasting in the fruit tree, Mawee, the leopard, came by. Now you know that leopards are enemies to all the animals of the forest. As Mawee came closer, the birds heard him say "I have wandered through this forest and found nothing to eat." When Mawee approached, he looked down at the bottom of the tree. There among the roots and leaves was a baby chick that had fallen to the ground. Mawee, being very hungry flung his claw at the baby bird, but missed. The tribe of birds, seeing what was happening, began to squeak and shrill and they dove down at the leopard. Mawee made every attempt to fight back, but could not overcome the tribe of birds. The leopard suffered at the strength of their numbers and had to retreat. The tribe of birds now were in charge of the forest. They had rescued their baby chick and defeated Mawee.

That night, the elder bird echoed to all the birds of African forest:

"Let us make music and dance and celebrate our ancestors. For in numbers we are strong, and for tonight, everything is right."

Makumba: the Story of the Mother Elephant

It was daybreak and early that morning Malik had plans to journey into the forest to search for food for his family. Malik was growing in stature and maturing into a great Mandinka tribesman. Both his physical and spiritual muscles were growing stronger. He had a good attitude and was faithful to serve his family and village.

Food was scarce in the village and Malik was hopeful to find meat for the cooking pot. Today he was setting traps in the dense forest to catch the swift moving guinea fowl, a bird about the size of a large chicken that has a good deal of tasty meat on it. Having seven wanting brothers, Malik would need to set several traps to gather enough meat for everyone.

Malik's first task was to find Hansa, a dark brown nut that is the favorite food of the guinea fowl. He used the Hansa as bait for his traps which he created from rope and nearby branches. Using his strong arms and legs, Malik climbed and then concealed himself in a nearby tree. After a short while, he heard the soft echo of kruh-kruh, kruh-kraaa coming from the bush. There was a flock of guinea fowl below and they had come to eat the hansa in the traps. Yes! - The hunt was successful. - Malik descended from the tree and collected his catch; he would not return home empty-handed. He put the birds into a sack and returned to his village knowing his family would feast on fresh meat that night.

After a hearty evening meal, the village festivities began. In two more days, the men of the tribe would go on a hunt for big game. This meat would be critical for the tribe's survival. There was music making and dancing around the camp fire. The men liked to dance to the sound of the drum so Malik drummed for them and created much merriment. Malik played his drum and talked to his ancestors. Through the sound of his music, he spoke to them:

Gone from us

   Out of sight

      Take me back

         To what's right

            Hear me now

               Come, bright light

                  Protect our ancient way of life.

Evening had now settled upon the village and the moonlight illuminated the night sky. Having stepped away from the campfire, the mosquitos were fierce. Malik hurried back to his hut, undressed himself and fell immediately into a deep sleep. He was awakened by a voice. There in front of him was an apparition of the wise elder Ykni calling to Malik:

> "Malik, Malik, I have heard the sounds of your drum. Wake up and take notice, for I have something very important to tell you. I have concern for our people. They have listened to the untruths of the world and there are forces working against them. They need a leader to teach them to believe in themselves and put a dream in their hearts. You must assemble our people; make them understand that they are destined for greatness, for out of greatness they come. The elders have been watching you, Malik. You have an important job to do! It won't be easy, but in the face of adversity, you will discover your true self. Do you understand that this is the charge you have been given by the elders?" Malik answered with much uncertainty, "I think I do."

Malik awakened the next morning with Ykni's message still imprinted upon his mind. His heart was heavy and he told himself, "I am but a young boy. How can I change the way our people think so they will love themselves and believe in the future of our village?" This was such an important task that Malik told himself, "I need the counsel of an old friend. I will seek out Makumba, matriarch of the elephant herd." She is a wise old elephant and it is believed at the beginning of creation, Makumba was taught the magic of the universe.

To find the elephant herd, Malik traveled deep into the jungle until the bush became very dense and he could hardly see. It was there he found Makumba. As Malik approached, Makumba swung around, flapping her ears to greet him. Her legs were the size of baobab trees, and she waved her trunk making a trumpeting sound. Makumba proceeded at a steady gait, moving along toward Malik. The excitement of Makumba seeing Malik was evident. She called to him "Greetings, young warrior. What brings boy-man here to see me?"

Malik responded saying "I come to seek your counsel. You are matriarch of the elephant herd, respected by all. You lead by example with understanding and fairness. I know you have always kept peace and harmony among the animals of the forest. As a leader of the land animals, you hold the knowledge of the ancient ways."

Malik then told Makumba about the vision of the elder and the prophecy that he would lead his people into greatness. "Ah" said Makumba "We are living in a time of chaos and instability. And you, little one, are destined to bring some truth and order to it all." Let me tell you a story from some time ago, in the Age of Despair.

The Age of Despair was a time of conflict between your people. Tribes were uprooted, moving from one dwelling place to another searching for food. There was hunger and famine everywhere. Vegetation was dying and the forest animals had no food. It had not rained for many days and the land was lifeless. It was then a great storm came. The sky was filled with fire as a dark shadow in the sky sent down a great arrow of brightness to pierce our land. That great arrow of brightness ignited a devastating fire in our forest which made the night seem as day. The lions, zebras, water buffalo, and giraffes moved quickly to escape the fire's path. The smaller creatures burrowed into the ground and under rocks for protection, while the birds flew away leaving their eggs and nests behind.

Now the family of elephants was led by the matriarch of the herd, Mother Elephant. She was wise, brave, and so strong that she could toss a lion into the brush with her trunk. Standing motionless in her tracks as she watched the burning fires in the distance, she determined her next steps. She counted her herd, even the small calves, took note of their surroundings and bellowed a warning sound. From all directions, elephant mommas and babies, and the male elephants lumbered toward Mother Elephant's reverberating bellow.

All the herd lined up single file behind her with the large bull elephants guarding the rear. The Elephant tribe followed the trumpeting sound of their leader as they trampled their way through the blazing forest, carving a clear path through the bush and trees. The ground like thunder shook and roared as the elephant herd moved toward the safety of the water, and all the elephants were spared from harm.

As the elephant herd pushed its way through the forest, Mother Elephant saw something moving in the bushes. She lowered her head, ready to attack if necessary. To her surprise there emerged a tribe of man creatures, slowly moving, frightened and stumbling along the thorny bush. They were far from their homes with no one to lead them along the way. Confused, tired, and wounded, many were unable to continue their journey on foot.

Mother Elephant thought for a moment, then she did something completely unexpected. She spoke to the man creatures saying "How terrified you must be, weak as you are and so far from home. We, the elephant herd, are the strongest and most compassionate animals of the jungle. Mother Elephant looked to her herd and commanded them to "Hold the line, be not afraid, be still and be gentle." With that, Mother Elephant lowered her body and offered the man creatures a ride on her back. She said, "Let us elephants carry your burden." Through this act of strength and kindness, the elephant herd and the man creatures became friends and allies.

Makumba finished her story and turned to Malik. "Now tell me, man-boy, what did you learn from this story?" Malik pondered for a moment and then responded:

> "You, Mother Elephant, have taught me the qualities of being a good leader. In the face of danger, a good leader studies the situation and commands the respect and authority to perform as needed. Leaders take care of their people and create safe havens for them. And you, Mother Elephant have taught your herd to be proud, responsible animals. A great leader gives their people something to believe in and live for.

Makumba said to Malik:

> *"Well done man-boy. Now go and do the same because the magic of the universe is that we are 'One' as living creatures and need to take care of each other."*

The Tortoise and the Garden

It had been a wonderful day for Malik. He and his brothers had gone on a hunting trip with the village men and the chief. Today, Malik could show his courage and his strength as a hunter. They would hunt for antelope, zebra, and the water buffalo. Throughout their journey, the hunters found the tracks of animals, but the animals had moved farther away from the village, deeper into the forest in search of food and water. At the end of the hunting day, the warriors returned to the village empty handed. Today the village men understood that they too may soon need to move farther into the forest to provide food for their village.

Still excited after their return from the hunt, Malik and his brothers wrestled about on the ground, pretending to be fearless warriors hunting the great lion. They told stories of the day and played warrior games, seeing who could jump the highest. It was late and the sun was preparing to rest. The nearby mountains cast their shadows over the village as if to protect the village from harm. Malik could hear the familiar sounds of the night. This night was special as the entire tribe would have dinner together around the fire. They would eat wild fruits and dried meat that had been stored from previous hunts.

When dinner was finished, it was time for the storytelling to begin. This night, the griot's story was about a wise man of long ago who could gaze into the heavens, at the sun, the moon, and the stars and predict future events. One night, while reading the stars, the Wise Man saw a star of great light. It was an unusual star, maybe a new star from the gods. This star was to guide him on a journey that would change the world forever. The Wise Man was to follow the star to the birthplace of a very special child.

He thought to himself, I need a special gift to give in honor of this child's birth. This gift must be of precious substance, something holy in nature. "I know" said the Wise Man, "Frankincense is a special oil that is used to bless and anoint the sick. It has a wonderful holy smell. This would be the perfect gift." He thought, I will go to the Horn of Africa and find the Boswellia sacra and Comiphor trees. I will cut their bark and scrape away the dried sap to prepare my offering to this child. So, the Wise Man packed food and water and set off on his camel to find the Frankincense to give to the blessed child.

Malik thought, what a splendid night this has been. The stars and moon brightened the heavens. My ancestors have bestowed great wisdom and goodness of heart. Indeed, I am blessed by their love and guidance. That night, Malik played his drum and talked to his ancestors through the sound of his music. He spoke to them:

Gone from us

    Out of sight

        Take me back

            To what's right

                Hear me now

                    Come, bright light

                        Protect our ancient way of life.

Malik returned to the refuge of his small hut remembering the griot's story. He fell into a deep sleep that night filled with commitment and love for his family and tribe. As before, Malik heard a voice, saying "I have heard the call of your drum." Malik looked up to see Ykni, an elder of the lost tribes of Africa. Malik said to the apparition "What have you come to tell me this time?"

Ykni said "I have come because I am worried about the future of our people. I have seen our hopes for prosperity die. Our resources have been depleted. Our farmland and forests are being burned. The spices and even the frankincense so treasured by our Wise Men will soon be gone. Our people have become collaborators in their own destruction. It is you Malik who must guide your people to the way of our ancestors. You have a light that radiates within you like the sun during the day and the North Star at night, and your people are calling to you.

Soon, the night passed and day broke. Malik awoke to the sound of his mother moving around in their hut. She was boiling water for tea over a small fire, and his younger brother had just brought in some fresh figs and yams for breakfast. Malik's mother had the responsibility of producing the meals for the family. Tilling the garden, planting the seeds, weeding, and harvesting the food consumed a good deal of her time. She was not feeling well that morning, so after breakfast, Malik ventured out to tend the family's garden. He took a cowhide bag full of water and a few beans to eat after his work was done. When he arrived at the garden, he saw that it was in shambles and many of the young seedlings and shoots were gone. An animal had been there nibbling on the plants, feeding all night long.

Now, the night before, the tortoise had climbed atop a log, when suddenly the log was pulled into the treacherous waters of the river. The tortoise clung to the log all night long, in the dark shadows of the snakes and crocodiles, hoping to get to the other side of the river.

When the tortoise finally reached land, he was very tired and hungry. Soon, the weary tortoise happened upon Malik's family garden. The vegetables, potatoes, yams, casava and cabbage looked very yummy. So, the tortoise helped himself to this bountiful feast.

Malik surveyed the garden area very carefully searching for the perpetrator; the one who had destroyed his family's garden. After finding some shallow digs under the bushes, he thought, I will wait until this animal comes out of its hide to warm up and eat and then I will catch it for my dinner. After a while, Malik could see the bushes move and was surprised to see a tortoise departing from its burrow. Malik called out to the tortoise "You have devoured my vegetables and have destroyed my crop. What shall I do to you?"

The tortoise responded "This garden is remarkable and the food is plentiful enough for everyone. I am claiming the rights to this garden under 'Oberhoheit.' I will fill my stomach, and what I do not eat, I will sell to the other animals of the forest." "It is I who am in charge of this garden now, and it is I who have ownership and power over it."

Malik, furious by what the tortoise said, responded "This is my family's soil, and we decide what is planted here and who shall profit from the crops planted. The land is very important to the life of my village and the land should be treated with respect. My people have been one with the land for many generations. It is a sustaining source from our Creator."

Malik then said to the tortoise "I will give you a challenge. If you win the challenge then you may take the land and the crops and do as you will with them. Surely you tortoise, would agree to this."

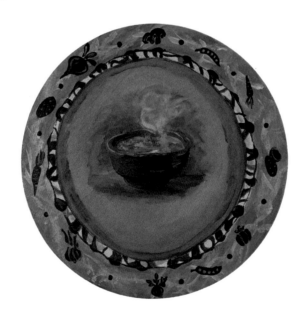

"And what would you have me do?" said the Tortoise. Malik said, "I will make a soup with the vegetables left in the garden. If you eat more soup than me, then the garden will become yours. I will even let you go first so that you can have as much soup as you want." Malik then proceeded to pluck the remaining vegetables and earthy spices from his garden. He chopped them up, mixed them with some creamy coconut milk, and cooked the soup over a slow fire.

The warm earthy aroma of the soup was too much for the tortoise to resist. The greedy tortoise filled his bowl of soup until there was no more in the pot for the young boy Malik to eat. After devouring all of the soup, the tortoise said "I have eaten all of the soup and there is none left for you, so I have won the challenge and will take your garden for myself." Malik said, "So you have."

Just then the beautiful fennec fox, with its bushy tail and beautiful large ears, came out of its den. The fox had been listening to the tortoise and was waiting underground until the tortoise had finished his soup. The tortoise having eaten all the soup, was unable to move and became easy prey for the fox. The tortoise pleaded with Mailik "Save me from the fox and the garden is yours." Malik responded to the tortoise "No, you have eaten all of the soup and have won the challenge." The fox then snatched the tortoise and pulled it down into his den, never to be seen again.

In the end, Malik had won the challenge. He had been taught by the great elders of his tribe, that man must not infringe upon the rules of nature in search of self-fulfillment and greed. He bellowed these words for all the animals to hear:

> *"Take heed my forest companions, all living creatures can co-exist and live abundantly. Surely, the Earth provides enough for all if we do not over-indulge. For greed brings forth an unbalanced society."*

Doobaloo, Khari and the Baby Chicks

Today was an ordinary day in the village. The sun was shining brightly, and Malik could hear the birds singing noisily outside his family's hut. His mother had a breakfast of fruit, nuts, and goat's milk waiting for the family. Malik was slow to get up because his muscles ached from yesterday's hard labor at clearing the field. Today, a new project awaited him. After breakfast, he, his father, and brothers would begin making plans to build a home for their newly purchased *akoho* or chickens.

The care and safety of the flock would be Malik's responsibility and this was a good project for him. A curious boy with a lot of creative energy, he was always thinking of new ideas and solutions to benefit the life of his family and the villagers. Malik's many ideas and plans to conjure his design for this new chicken coop sprang from his ability to understand the ways of nature and its jungle elements. First though, he would need to seek out the advice of his father and the wisdom of the elders.

He thought, we will build the chicken coop under the shade of the trees so that the trees will soften the heat of the African sun. Malik could picture the coop looking like a beehive. He would weave the grass thatch together in small bundles and attach the bundles to the framework of the roof. His brothers would need to cut many branches to support the heavy weight of the thatched bundles on the roof. The raised bamboo floor would help keep the chicken coop clean. Windows and doors made out of bamboo slats would allow lots of fresh air to flow through the hut. There would be a reed fence surrounding the chicken coop made from bundles of elephant grass which would help protect the flock, especially the new chicks from predators like rats, snakes, mongoose, hawks, and foxes.

Inside the chicken coop, a wooden feeder would be suspended from the roof so those pesky rats would not run off with their food. There would be baskets for the hens to nest in and perches on which they could roost. The baby chicks would be warm and dry as they sleep in the nest with their mother hen at night. The flock's vigilant roosters would guard the nests and protect them from the dangerous predators.

Malik's brain had been buzzing all day long with thoughts of the chicken coop. He had conceptualized all of the key components and his plans were coming into place. That night, feeling overwhelmed and fatigued, he embraced the quiet sounds of the jungle and the peacefulness of the circle around the campfire. Sitting on the rough grass mat, with the soft sound of the night breeze in the air, Malik drummed in rhythm to the rustling leaves of the trees. He spoke to his ancestors, saying:

Gone from us

    Out of sight

        Take me back

            To what's right

                Hear me now

                    Come, bright light

                        Protect our ancient way of life.

Malik's thoughts drifted in space until time seemed to completely stop as he was finally lulled into a deep sleep. In his dream world, the elder Ykni came to him. Ykni spoke to Malik saying "I am concerned about our children and the future of our people. The world is not safe for our young ones. Our leaders have forced them to live in a hostile society. They are neither welcomed nor safe. Danger is lurking everywhere. If this does not change, there will be unfortunate consequences for all of mankind." Malik was so disturbed by this foretelling, that it caused him to drift in and out of his sleep that night. It was a night that he would not soon forget.

The next morning, Malik was awakened by the sound of the monkeys as they called out to one another. The dew was still heavy on the grass and the sunrise was spectacular. It beckoned to Malik, giving him energy. There was a mystic rhythm to the breeze as Malik and his brothers began the task of building their new chicken coop. The day seemed to stretch on as they built the thatched hut, cutting many poles to support the roof. The sun was feverishly hot and the work was hard. As the day faded, so did their energy. With darkness setting in, the finishing touches would need to wait until the next day.

The following morning, Malik's father brought his flock of chickens to the village. They were accompanied by two magnificent roosters. One of the roosters was a grand spectacle with striking plumage of mahogany color and a large black comb at the top of his head. He was a very proud fellow and could make a crowing sound loud enough to wake the entire village. This black rooster was called Khari (meaning kingly), and his family came from greatness. Khari's family coat of arms was a symbol of power and pride. He cared very much for his family of chickens, and pledged to the mother hens and baby chicks that he would love them, protect them, and keep them safe from all harm. He would never desert or shirk his responsibilities of guarding the chicken coop.

The second rooster, fat, lazy, and wearing a garment of white fluff tinted with black spots and a large red comb on the top of his head, was called Doobaloo (meaning one who doesn't work). This self-indulgent rooster was arrogant and prideful and enjoyed hearing the loud shrill of his own crowing. Noted for his bad temperament and presumptuous attitude, he was often absent when most needed in the flock and would take a holiday whenever he fancied.

In the nearby jungle, there lived a gargantuan rat named Riki. Riki belonged to the rat family and was an untrustworthy scavenger and predator by nature who would devour virtually anything, including baby chicks. The rat family was the natural enemy of the chicken family, so the chicken family considered Riki evil and the vermin of the village.

One day, Riki, the rat approached Doobaloo, the rooster, and said "Dear Friend, it is not good that our families quarrel, and I want there to be peace among us. I would like for there to be a closer relationship between your chicken family and my rat family. To improve our relationship, I should like to offer my services to you and help guard your chicken coop. You are a fine rooster but staying awake all night and being sleep-deprived is below your station in life. I will take the night guard while you get your much-needed sleep. You can be assured I will call you when there is a predator nearby or when a situation escalates that I cannot handle."

"Also, each night I will bring to you a bag of magical grain from the fields of the Mandinka tribesmen. The hardy flavor will not only fill your belly, but it will give you incredible strength and power. In exchange for guarding your chicken coop and giving you this magical grain, I will need something in return. Each evening, after guarding your chicken coop, I will take two baby chicks with me. I will raise them as my own and teach them the ways of the rats. When they are grown and have learned our ways, I will return them to you."

Now, Riki the rat had no intention of returning the baby chicks to their families. His plan was to hide the chicks away and fatten them up so that at just the right time, he would consume them for a delectable evening meal. Doobaloo the rooster, thinking about this opportunity to slumber throughout his watch and then have a fine meal of grain for his morning breakfast was overjoyed at the rat's proposition and foolishly agreed for Riki to guard the chicken coop. His greed was blind, and he had negotiated with Riki the rat for the baby chicks.

That night after the sun melted into the sky, Riki the rat came to his post at the chicken coop. Riki, very quietly, searched around the coop and found a crack in the floor to enter the hut. The hens and chicks were sound asleep. He crept over to Mother Hen Eshe's nest and grabbed two of her little chicks. Without a sound, he tucked them away in his pouch and ran back through the hole in the floor. At the crack of dawn Doobaloo the rooster arrived to make his morning rounds and to crow in the new day. Riki the rat, having fulfilled his promise, quickly gave Doobaloo, the rooster his share of the magical grain and scampered off into the jungle.

When the sun broke, the hens were ready to be fed and take their chicks out to learn a lesson on scavenging for food. Mother Hen Eshe, counted her chicks "One, Two, Three. Oh-no, where have two of my chicks gone?" She was frantic and quickly ran to Doobaloo to ask if he had seen her babies. Doobaloo responded to Eshe, "Well, I talked to your little ones last night. They went into the bush to explore the jungle. I am sure that when they get hungry and tired, they will return to your nest. I know that your faith is strong. Have patience and you will see them again soon."

The next evening, Riki the rat returned to the chicken coop after the hens were asleep. Same as the night before, Riki, crept into the coop and helped himself to two more little chicks. And again, the next morning, Doobaloo the rooster ate the magical grain and like clockwork crowed in the morning sun as Riki the rat scampered off into the jungle with the two chicks.

Just then, Doobaloo the rooster heard a screech from the chicken coop. This time, it was Mother Hen, Kagisho. She could not find two of her little chicks anywhere. She asked what might have happened to them. "Well," Doobaloo the rooster said, "Your little chicks were sold to a neighbor. They are very strong little fellows and can contribute to that farmer's economy. As soon as they finish their tasks, the neighbor will return them to you. Our neighbor is a good man and your little chicks will be well taken care of. Do not worry, you will see them again soon".

Now, Khari, the black rooster, had been put in charge of another chicken coop. When Khari heard the news of the missing baby chicks, he realized time was not on his side, and he would need to work quickly to bring the chicks home safely. His first order of investigation was to find out if any of the jungle animals could provide clues about the baby chicks disappearance. He went straight to the source of the bush to talk to the alpha chimp, Rashidi (meaning good council) to inquire about their disappearance. He asked Rashidi if he had seen any baby chicks wandering about in the jungle. Rashidi thought for a moment and then responded saying "I think I smell a rat in the chicken coop."

Now the chimps were building their nests in the trees above the bush and one of the chimps had seen Riki the rat scurrying back to his burrow early in the morning.

He was carrying a pouch with him and seemed very nervous. Hearing this, Rashidi sent his team of chimp detectives to investigate. They used their digging sticks to excavate the underground nest of Riki the rat. There in the home of Riki were the four baby chicks.

With this information, Rashidi called a tribal court of chimpanzees and other members of the jungle alliance. There was a spectrum of animals represented from across the land, including zebras, leopards, lions, macaws, anaconda, gorillas, rhinos, elephants, giraffes, and more. They were there to review the facts and determine innocence or guilt of the accused Riki the rat. Having the chimps' testimony along with the proof of evidence (the baby chicks), there was a quick deliberation and they presented a verdict of "guilty." They called for the conviction of Riki the rat and sentenced him to the "Circle of Truth." The alliance of jungle animals formed a closely-knit circle around Riki the rat while the chimpanzees, in their nests above, threw small sticks at Riki. He cried out and begged for forgiveness. Riki pledged to make amends to the flock of chickens and agreed to never again oppress or harm another animal. With that, the council let Riki go.

The baby chicks were then given to the care of Khari, the black rooster who led them safely back home. For Doobaloo's participation in this crime against their flock, the mother hens barred him from the village and the chicken coop. He was exiled to lands beyond the jungle, never to be seen again. A small present of grain was wrapped in cloth and presented to Khari, not in payment, but in recognition of his service to the chicken flock. He was granted guardianship over the chicken coop and through his vigilance he protected the offspring of those chickens for generations to come.

> *Creation is a miracle and life is the most precious resource we have. We live in troubled times and our future hinges on the wellbeing of our children. Keep them safe and empower them, for they will save us.*

Taroo the Crow and the Stones of Wisdom

Winter is upon Malik's village; the air is dry and sunshine abounds. By the river, the crocodiles and hippos are basking in the warm waters. The birds are in abundance and their silhouettes are like strands of garland against the deep blue sky. The beetles are humming and the doves coo from the branches above. Crows are lighting on the newly picked fields searching for grubs while in the dense foliage there is a venomous viper waiting to capture his morning breakfast.

The hue of dawn has unfolded upon the village. Just like every other day, Malik and his brothers are awakened by their mother's call to breakfast. Instead of getting up, Mother's soothing soft voice had a way of luring Malik back into a gentle second sleep. Eventually, the smell of freshly made fish soup aroused his spirits and he clumsily sat up on his bed. It was then he remembered that today the brothers would travel through the jungle to visit Maada, Malik's grandfather.

In the past Maada was the adviser to one of their great chiefs. Wise and brave, he was a great Mandinka warrior and he knew well the ways of their ancestors. Winter was now upon Maada and his illness was like a bitter, unyielding wind impelling his spirit.

Word about Maada's sickness was delivered by the winged messenger, a black crow named Taroo (meaning quick or fast). Taroo, the Master Crow circled above Malik's head and cried out saying, "It is I, Taroo. My feathers are black as night. I can soar above the land and I see everything. You can look into my eyes and see images of what is to come. I have a beautiful black tail and can sing and dance. Caw, caw. Look at me! I have a message regarding your grandfather, Maada. He is calling for prayers and wants to meet with his grandsons before he goes for a walk into the spirit world."

Hearing Taroo's message, that next morning, the boys set out on their journey to Maada's home, taking with them spears for hunting, some dried meats, and vessels of water. Along the way, not far from the village, Malik and his brothers passed the ancient burial mounds of their tribal kings and chiefs. This sacred place is where Malik would sometimes go to be by himself, to meditate, and find harmony with his ancestors. Here, he felt close to nature and the great Mother Earth; here energy was in abundance. Oftentimes he would find ancient arrows, knives, and spearheads, washed from the ground by the rain, but he would always leave them for fear of disturbing his ancestors' resting place. The lifeblood of their ancestors was significant to tribal culture, as was this trip for the boys to pay respect to their grandfather. Therefore, Malik brought with him his drum in hopes of receiving his grandfather's blessing.

When Malik and his brothers arrived at Maada's farm, they first went to the river to bathe and cleanse themselves for their visit with grandfather. They found their grandmother on the path waiting for them. She had made some wonjo juice from dried hibiscus flowers and sugar and gave it to the boys to quench their thirst. The evening meal was already prepared so after their bath, they journeyed on to Maada's hut where he was waiting and greeted them with blessings. The food was on the table, and they ate until their rumbling bellies were filled.

After dinner, they gathered around the crackling campfire. Maada, speaking to the boys said, "Each of you has done well and bring me much happiness. You have been brought up from childhood to be great warriors. I have gifts of honor for each of you. I give to you a goat and a bag of seeds from my garden." Maada had gathered all kinds of herbs and vegetable seeds from his garden and gave one bag of seeds to each of his grandsons. He told them they must plant a garden when they return home. The seeds would provide nourishment for future generations of Mandinka warriors.

The boys grew tired as the day had quickly darkened into night. Maada said "Now, come close so that you may hear my words. You, my grandsons, are of equal strength so I give to each of you the same authority in life. However, there is one of you with knowledge of truths yet untold; he brings to me great pleasure." Having said that, Maada dismissed the seven brothers but asked Malik to stay a bit longer with him. That night, Maada told Malik stories of his youth as a Mandinka warrior, the beauty and devastation of the African jungle through times of peace and war, love and hatred, drought and sickness, abundance and healing.

The young Malik loved his grandfather very much and sought to please him. He said to Maada, "I will stay close and attend to your duties. Tell me what you need." Maada said to Malik "I feel weak and my heart beats so strangely. I need nothing but to hear you drum for me." With a loving spirit, Malik drummed to the rhythmic pulse of his grandfather's heart. He spoke to his ancestors, saying:

Gone from us

　Out of sight

　　Take me back

　　　To what's right

　　　　Hear me now

　　　　　Come, bright light

　　　　　　Protect our ancient way of life.

When Maada and Malik withdrew to their hut, slumber quickly came upon them. As the night passed, Ykni and the elders materialized and made their appearance known. A voice called to Maada and Malik. Maada's eyes opened and in his confused state of mind he saw thirteen stately figures. There was a mist, a fog around them. You could tell that they held a higher level of existence as the light flowed through their bodies. They wore beautifully embroidered tunics with ornamental sashes and looked of great importance. Maada's heart thumped loudly as he spoke to the spirits saying "I know you. You are Ykni and the elders who hold the wisdom of our ancient ways." Tears welled up in Maada's eyes at the sight of these great teachers and healers.

Ykni, the chief elder responded as he turned to Malik, saying "In the ancient days, all mankind dwelt together in one place and they lived in peace and were happy. We need to return to the ways of those before us. Malik, this evening you will receive your inheritance from us." Ykni was holding a large goatskin sack in his hands, and one by one, each of the twelve elders pulled out a stone from the bag. On each stone was written words of knowledge and wisdom from their African ancestors.

And they began reading the words of understanding to Malik and his grandfather.

1. *We know our Creator through the gifts we receive so start each day with a prayer of gratitude.*

2. *Body, mind, and soul together leads us to a path of self-discovery.*

3. *The pendulum swings back. Be loyal to your people. Restoration and destiny is ours to claim.*

4. *You come from greatness - You are greatness.*

5. *Plant your roots deeply. Love and protect your family.*

6. *Always seek out wisdom, for in wisdom you will find life.*

7. *Your most formidable enemy lies within you. Keep your heart and mind pure.*

8. *Be honorable and have courage; treat others with respect and understanding*

9. *The truth does not belong to one person. It is for everyone to hear. We must learn to tell our story, our truth.*

10. *Listen more and speak less and the wisdom of the ages will lead you onward.*

11. *Surround yourself with those of good heart; people who fill you up.*

12. One cannot choose how life begins, but one can choose how to live life.

Malik responded to the elders "I pray that I am worthy of this birthright. I have been empowered to pass on the knowledge of our ancestors, to reconnect with our ancestral traditions, keeping alive the ways of those who have gone before us."

Then the elders turned toward Maada and said "Our eyes have looked upon you and have seen your struggles. We know that your strength is fading and that you long for your Creator. In all that you have done, you have been strong, yet gentle and honorable in all your dealings. From birth, you were granted skills with the spear and bow, and you have always seen that your people had food and were protected. Now it is our time to take care of you."

Maada's face was pale and his breathing became more rapid. He was covered in sweat from a fever and had lost so much weight that his skin clung to his bones. Trying to pull enough air out of his lungs, he finally let out a deep breath. His voice quivered as he spoke to the elders. "I have had a good life and done my best. I belong to the Creator now and long to be with my ancestors." The elders responded to Maada, saying "I know that you grow weary, but the time has not yet come for your departure."

Then the elders called out to the beasts of the jungle to come to Maada, their master. They were to bring herbs and spices from the jungle that had secret healing powers. The animals would create an herbal potion that would restore Maada's body and make him well again.

The ground shook as the beasts made their way to Maada's hut, and like a great king, the Lion was the first to approach. He came and bowed before Maada. Then he stopped at the great black vessel over the campfire and dropped some olives into the brew. Maada's heart would become healthier with the use of this olive oil. Then the other jungle animals fell into step behind the Lion. They each knew what to do without communicating with each other. The Dwarf Crocodile brought a clove of garlic for the brew. The garlic's oils would keep Maada's lungs clear of infections. The Elephant brought some ginger root to warm him and reduce his inflammation. The Baboon brought Sweet Flag, a root that had antibiotic properties. One by one all the animals came with their herbs and spices as gifts for Maada.

As the brew simmered over the fire, the smell of the herbs and spices was almost overpowering. When the animals had completed their tasks and the brew was ready, the elders scooped a full cup from the pot and gave it to Maada. As he drank the healing potion something came alive in his body. The blood rushed to his face and slowly the warmth reddened his cheeks. He took in deep wonderful breaths as the jungle night air filled his lungs. As Maada stood up, he seemed to grow taller, feeling his strength return to his body. He felt a new sense of hope. There was confidence once again in his stature.

Maada thanked the elders and the creatures of the jungle for their gifts of love. The red embers were now gone from the fire, and they all stood in silence for a moment. As the elders watched Maada return to the living, they offered prayers of gratitude to the Creator for his healing. Then the elders and the beasts of the jungle departed as quickly as they had appeared. Their tasks were complete. As the darkness began to lift, so did the dawning of a splendid new day. Maada had been healed and the seeds of wisdom had been planted in Malik's mind. Everything was as it should be.

In the bleak light of the morning, the brothers bid their farewells to Maada and their grandmother. They were sad to leave their grandfather and slowly descended the path toward their village with a heavy heart. They journeyed on crossing small creeks and pathways, until at the edge of the forest they happened upon a river. It was midday, and tired from their journey, the brothers set up camp under the trees to escape the blistering sun.

Hearing noises from the trees above, Malik said to his brothers "Those who are calling to us, who are they?" Looking up, Malik and his brothers see crows circling above, and perched in the Baobab or Wisdom tree they see Master Crow, Taroo. Malik called to Taroo and asked to speak to him.

Taroo flew down to Malik and said, "I know you, Malik. I have seen the elders' presence in your life and you are destined for great things. You are to teach your people their history. They must learn to be proud and strong. You are to return to your father's village and plant the seeds that Maada has given you, seeds to sustain your body. Also, plant the seeds of truth from Ykni and the elders, seeds for your people to live by to sustain their hearts and minds. You have been given a heavy weight of responsibility. Now that you have learned the truth, you must clear the path and make way for the future of your people."

In this spirit, the crows now have a kinship with your human family, and we have strength in numbers. We are your tribe; wise, brave, and swift. It is our duty to keep you safe. You won't always see us, but we will be hiding in the trees above you, ready to warn you and protect your people from predators. We will sacrifice our lives to save yours. Always know, that like your ancestors, our life forces cannot be separated, so whatever befalls you, befalls us.

Malik thanked the crows for their loyalty and the boys then continued their travel homeward with a soft winter wind at their backs. He knew that the eyes of the jungle were upon him, and he could hear their voices calling his name. He had become their leader now. Malik knew that for the future of his people and their homeland in Africa, there would be many challenges and great battles ahead of them. However, they would always have the wisdom of their ancestors to lead the way.

We must plant seeds of nourishment for both mind and body. Truth flows through our history and the lifeblood of our ancestors, paving the way to new beginnings.

Printed in the United States
by Baker & Taylor Publisher Services